I'M BROWN aND I'M SMart

WRItten by
SHerrita Berry-Pettus M.Ed

ILLUStrated by
JoHaNNe IMMiS .

D1402083

Copyright © 2017 by Sherrita Berry-Pettus M.Ed/ Books by Mrs.Berry-Pettus
All rights reserved. No part of this book may be reproduced, scanned,
or distributed in any printed or electronic form without permission.
First Edition: March 3, 2017
Printed in the United States of America
ISBN: 978-1-945342-06-6

Hi I'M AHMari...and I'M broWN and.. .I'M SMart!

My SKiN iS broWN LiKe a bear. I'M JuSt aS
StroNg you KNoW.

My eyes are brown and strong.

I love Working With Numbers!

I can count all the way to 100! All because...

I'm brown and I'm smart!

My MOMMy is
CHOCOLAte brown
and SHe is a teacher.

My MOMMy teLLS Me every day.

Loving and believing in yourself is important.

Once you love self, you can love all others.

I Love My MOM. I Love My dad!
I Love My brothers!

I love my Aunties.

I love my Uncle!

I love my whole family!

I have all of this love to share...
all because I love myself!

At Night beFore I go to bed,
I LOOK iN the MirrOr and Say ....

I Love MySeLF.

I aM very SMart.

I Love My broWN SKiN.

THEN I think about HOW SMART I AM
and WHAT I love to do...

I love WORKiNG WiTH SHAPeS and
playing NeW games!

I am thankful to be WHO I am!

WHO's brown
and proud?

I am!

WHO'S brown and smart?

I am....

and you KNOW What.....
So are you!

BUILDING CONFIDENT SCHOLARS THROUGH LITERACY

Mrs. Berry-Pettus

Thank you for your support! If you like this book, please check out my other books.

www.booksbymrsberry-pettus.com

Teaching
all children
that they are
PERFECT
exactly the
way they are!

Smile Bright
·Chocolate Prince·

I'M BROWN
and
I'M SMART

Rock On With Your
Afro Puffs!

I'm
Brown
and
I'm
Pretty!

Books make
great gifts!

The Marvelous
World
of
Shapes
by
Sherrita Berry-Pettus, M.Ed.

Illustrations
by
James Thomas

FOLLOW ON SOCIAL MEDIA!

 @mrs.berry-pettus   @mrsberrypettus

 @mrsberrypettus

39984621R10015

Made in the USA
Middletown, DE
22 March 2019